MONSTER HIGH™

MONSTER RESCUE

GO GET LAGOONA!

MONSTER HIGH

MONSTER RESCUE

GO GET LAGOONA!

BY MISTY VON SPOOKS

(L)(B)

LITTLE, BROWN AND COMPANY
New York Boston

Cover design by Véronique Lefèvre Sweet.
Cover illustration by Yulia Rumyantseva.

Little, Brown and Company
Hachette Book Group
1290 Avenue of the Americas, New York, NY 10104
Visit us at lb-kids.com
Visit monsterhigh.com

First Edition: April 2017

Little, Brown and Company is a division of Hachette Book Group, Inc. The Little, Brown name and logo are trademarks of Hachette Book Group, Inc.

The publisher is not responsible for websites (or their content) that are not owned by the publisher.

Library of Congress Control Number 2016951196

ISBNs: 978-0-316-31577-7 (hardcover), 978-0-316-31573-9 (ebook)

Printed in the United States of America

LSC-C

10 9 8 7 6 5 4 3 2 1

CHAPTER 1

Stop!" Draculaura suddenly cried. She yanked her hands off the Skullette right as it began to glow with pink light. Luckily, Draculaura's ghoulfriends—Frankie Stein, Clawdeen Wolf, and Cleo de Nile—followed her lead and let go of the Skullette just in time.

"Drac, what's wrong?" Frankie asked. "I thought we were on our way to find Lagoona."

"Yeah...we *were*," Draculaura said slowly.

"So what's the holdup?" asked Clawdeen,

pushing her thick hair away from her face. "My curls are about to be as dried up as those old mummies. Time to *go*!" None of the ghouls were fans of the relentless desert heat, but it seemed to hit Clawdeen even harder than the others.

"I think we need to go back to Monster High first," Draculaura explained. "We should check in with my dad. You know how much he worries about us. He probably thinks we're mummified by now!"

"True." Frankie laughed, nodding. Her dangling lightning-bolt earrings flashed in the sun.

"And we should probably learn more about where Lagoona lives," Draculaura continued. "We can't just keep dashing off without doing our homework, if you know what I mean."

"I think we've all learned our lesson on that one," Clawdeen said. "We definitely need to find out more about her location. What if we need special gear or stuff like that?"

"If we learned anything from our trip to the desert, it's that we've got to be prepared for just about anything," added Frankie.

"What do you think?" Draculaura said as she turned to Cleo. They'd all met Cleo for the first time just minutes before, and Draculaura didn't want her newest ghoulfriend to feel left out. "Do you mind if we take a detour to Monster High before we start searching for Lagoona?"

"Mind? Are you kidding?" Cleo replied. "That sounds golden. You know I've been positively *dying* to get to Monster High!"

"Fangtastic!" Draculaura cheered. She leaned down to pick up the Skullette again. As all the ghouls rested their fingertips against the Skullette, Draculaura closed her eyes. "*Monster High. Exsto monstrum.*"

Whoosh!

A tremendous swirling wind swept around the ghouls; at first, Draculaura thought the sands circling them might be a tornado, but then she realized that it was just the Skullette's enchantment at work. Then all of a sudden, the monsters found themselves on the front lawn of Monster High.

Draculaura gazed up at the school in amazement. It was not so long ago that the enormous mansion wasn't a school at all. It had started out as her home—or, more accurately, her hiding place. Ever since the great monster Fright Flight, Draculaura's dad, Dracula, had insisted that they hide from humans, or Normies, for their own protection. All the other monsters had gone into hiding too. It wasn't so bad for the first few centuries. But as the ages passed, Draculaura grew lonely for ghoulfriends of her very own.

Then, on the night of Draculaura's very first

flying lesson, everything had changed. Another monster, Frankie, who was just as eager for ghoulfriends as Draculaura was, had spotted her. The two ghouls had hit it off instantly, which had inspired Draculaura's most fangtastic idea ever: a school just for monsters, a place where they could finally come out of the shadows and make new friends. It wasn't enough to renovate the big, old house, though. To truly be a monstrous success, Monster High would need students—and lots of them. That's how Frankie and Draculaura found Clawdeen. With help from Frankie, Draculaura posted a message on the Monster Web. She hoped that at least one or two other monsters would respond.

To Draculaura's surprise, the response was overwhelming! Monsters all over the world were hoping to come out of hiding. And Monster High was where they wanted to do it. As their messages flooded Draculaura's inbox, she vowed to rescue each and every one. With the powerful Monster Mapalogue and its enchanted Skullette, Draculaura and her ghoulfriends had the ability to go anywhere in the whole wide world to find the monsters who were so eager to attend Monster High. The Mapalogue wasn't perfect, though. It transported the ghouls near where they needed to be—and the rest was up to them. A wild trip to the desert had led them to rescue Cleo de Nile, an Egyptian princess who'd been trapped in her tomb for a whole millennia. Next on the list was a monster named Lagoona Blue. But just before they used the Skullette to transport them to Lagoona's homeland, Draculaura realized that they needed to stop by Monster High.

Drac glanced anxiously at Cleo, wondering what she thought of her new school. She tried to see Monster High, from the towers and turrets to the sweeping staircases and arched doorways, through Cleo's eyes. *It's big—but is it pyramid-big?* Draculaura wondered. *Cleo's a royal ghoul who's spent her entire life surrounded by the ultimate luxuries. What will we do if she thinks Monster High is a disappointment?*

Draculaura didn't have to wonder for very long. Cleo beamed as she stared up at the huge mansion. "It's so cute!" she exclaimed. Her gold bangles clinked as she clapped her hands with excitement. "Which floor is mine?"

"Floor?" Draculaura echoed. "Um...nobody has her own floor. But the dorm rooms are pretty fangtastic!"

"Oh. Dorm rooms. Of course," Cleo said, trying to laugh off her mistake. "Why didn't I think of that?"

"Come on," Draculaura said, linking arms with her newest ghoulfriend. "Let's go inside. I can't wait to show you everything!"

"And I absolutely can't wait for a Mummy Mocha," Clawdeen added as she and Frankie fell into step beside them.

As the ghouls approached the front door, it swung open with an earsplitting *cre-e-e-e-ak*. Dracula stood in the doorway. "You're back!" he exclaimed, barely able to conceal his relief. "Come in, come in—and welcome!"

"Dad, please meet our newest student, Cleo de Nile," Draculaura said. Then she turned to Cleo. "This is my dad. Also known as the headmaster of Monster High."

"Well, now, I never expected that we'd be hosting royalty. It's an honor, your highness!" Dracula said as he bowed jokingly. However, it seemed to Cleo that there was nothing joking about it.

Cleo nodded regally to acknowledge Dracula. "You are very welcome," she replied. "I know you haven't had much time to prepare for my arrival, so I'd be happy to discuss my requirements with the head servant after he or she has unpacked my suitcase."

Uh-oh, Draculaura thought. *Is she for real?*

From the look on Frankie's face, Draculaura knew she wasn't the only one concerned.

"Uh—" Dracula began, momentarily speechless. "We don't have any servants here."

"But your ghoulfriends will be happy to help you unpack!" Frankie said brightly.

"Oops," Cleo said with a nervous laugh. "Thanks, ghouls. That's even better!"

"Mr. D.!" Clawdeen exclaimed. "You will not believe what happened when we went back to the desert!"

"I want to hear everything," he replied. "Let's fire up the Mummy Mocha machine."

"*Mmm*, that sounds ugh-mazing! I'll take mine with an extra drizzle of chocolate syrup. And not too much ice—that's very important," Cleo announced.

Everyone turned to look at her.

"Well, we actually make our own Mummy Mochas here," Draculaura explained.

Cleo blinked in surprise. "You *do?*" she asked in astonishment. "You make them *yourself?* But *how?*"

"It's easy!" Frankie assured her. "I'll teach you."

Dracula led them to the Creepeteria, where the Mummy Mocha machine was set up in the corner.

"These are the controls," Frankie explained as Cleo looked on gamely. "It's all very self-explanatory. Just program in whatever you'd like to drink and—"

"I got this!" Cleo interrupted as she squinted her kohl-rimmed eyes to read the options. "I cannot wait to practice all these, what do you call them? 'Do-It-Yourself' projects." Then she confidently punched a few of the buttons on the control panel. The Mummy Mocha machine rumbled to life, clanking and hissing as it prepared her drink.

"Oh! I almost forgot!" Cleo cried suddenly. "I like my Mummy Mochas made with extra-hot chocolate syrup poured over four and a half ice cubes!"

"I wouldn't—" Frankie began.

But it was too late; Cleo was already jabbing the buttons, trying to reprogram her order. The machine started to shake. A terrible groaning noise filled the Creepeteria.

"Take cover!" Frankie yelled.

Draculaura and the ghouls dove under a table and covered their heads.

Boom!

The doors on the Mummy Mocha machine burst open as a fountain of chocolate goop exploded out of the machine! Drops of chocolate rained over the Creepeteria while the ghouls shrieked in alarm!

Then silence filled the room.

Slowly, cautiously, the ghouls peeked out from under the table. A plume of smoke unfurled from the Mummy Mocha machine as a gooey river of chocolate syrup spread across the tiled floor.

"Uh-oh," Clawdeen finally said.

Cleo swallowed hard. "I'm sorry, ghouls. I, uh, guess I still have a lot to learn," she said.

Draculaura wrapped her arm around Cleo's shoulders. "We all do," she said. "That's why we're here!"

"And now seems like a good time to get started," Dracula announced. He crossed the room, carefully dodging the puddles of chocolate syrup, and reached into the broom closet. From the twinkle in his eye, Draculaura could tell that her dad wasn't really upset, even though the ghouls had managed to mess up the brand-new Creepeteria right after they'd returned.

"Frankie, would you take a look at the machine?" Dracula continued. "I hope it won't be too hard to repair."

"On it!" Frankie replied.

Then Dracula handed out the mops. There was one for Draculaura, one for Clawdeen, and even one for Cleo. Cleo hesitated before she took it. "So you just...push it around the floor?" she asked doubtfully.

"A little soap helps too," Draculaura said cheerfully. But instead of a *little* soap, she squirted a bit too much on the floor. Soon the Creepeteria was filled with floating bubbles, which made the ghouls laugh as they mopped up the mess.

Frankie finished fixing the Mummy Mocha machine before the other ghouls finished cleaning up the mess—which meant the minute they put away the mops, she was ready for them. "Who's thirsty?" she asked as she held out a tray with four perfect Mummy Mochas topped with whipped scream.

"Worth the wait," Clawdeen said, sighing after her first sip.

Cleo reached up to pop one last bubble that was floating overhead. "I honestly can't believe it," she said. "Frankie fixed the Mummy Mocha machine all by herself—and the rest of us *cleaned* the *floor*! I feel like we can do *anything*!"

"Speaking of anything…" Draculaura began.

The other ghouls turned to look at her.

"What should we do to get ready for Lagoona's rescue?" Drac continued.

"The possibilities are endless," Clawdeen said.

"And so are the risks," added Frankie. "We know practically nothing about Lagoona—or her location."

"That just means we've got a lot to learn," Draculaura said.

"Lucky for us, we're in the right place," joked Frankie.

Draculaura grinned at her friends. Thanks to Monster High, the ghouls had the chance to learn everything they needed to know—and school hadn't even started yet!

CHAPTER 2

Far, far away, the sun had just begun to rise, casting a faint pink light over the deserted beach. It was Lagoona Blue's favorite time of day, the only time when she could leave the ocean and explore the sandy shore as much as she wanted. But as soon as the sun was up, Lagoona had no choice but to dive deep, deep, deep into the water. That's when the tourists with their big cameras and the locals with their surfboards would flood the beach. Lagoona had heard enough stories about the great monster Fright Flight to understand why she had to stay far away from Normies.

But that didn't mean she had to like it.

Lagoona worked quickly, moving from dune to dune as she posted her signs: WARNING. TROPICAL CYCLONE APPROACHING. AVOID THE OCEAN UNTIL FURTHER NOTICE.

Lagoona didn't sign her name, of course, but she always left her mark. At the very bottom of the sign, she had added her favorite doodle: a curlicue wave that was about to crest. Lagoona added the symbol everywhere she could. It was even in her e-mail signature.

Lagoona had no idea if the Normies would pay attention to her warnings, but she certainly hoped so. The tropical cyclone that was brewing far out to sea was big—and that meant it was bad. If it veered off its current course, things would be fine. Sea creatures, after all, knew how to handle tropical cyclones—even the worst ones. But if it continued toward land? Lagoona knew in her heart that there wasn't a single Normie in the world who could handle the ferocious winds and monstrously big waves a tropical cyclone could cause.

Lagoona glanced warily at the sky. The pink color had deepened; it wouldn't be long until the golden sun popped up, sending her back to the deepest depths until tomorrow. She started to move even faster, racing against the inevitable sunrise.

"One…more…sign…" Lagoona muttered under her breath. If she listened closely, she could hear a car engine approaching. She shoved the sign-post into the sand and ran as fast as she could back to the ocean, just as the first beachgoers appeared at the edge of the dunes. Had they seen her? Lagoona wasn't sure, and she wasn't about to wait around to find out. In truth, though,

Lagoona wasn't too worried about it. With her light-blue skin and voluminous blond curls, it was easy for Lagoona to blend in to the sand and the sea when she needed to. Besides, the Normies were almost certainly too interested in checking out the waves to notice the sea ghoul slip into the ocean.

As the daughter of a sea monster, Lagoona knew how lucky she was; she could breathe just as easily underwater as she could on land. That meant that she could enjoy the best of both worlds whenever she wanted—as long as she stayed out of sight of the Normies. She smiled to herself as she glided through the water. If Normies ever caught sight of her iridescent scales, they wouldn't believe their eyes!

Lagoona didn't surface again until she'd reached the underwater grotto where she lived with her family, the only other sea monsters in the Great Barrier Reef. It wasn't *quite* as lonely as it sounded. Lagoona was friends with the other sea creatures in the Great Barrier Reef, even a giant squid who was just as misunderstood by the Normies as Lagoona and her family were. There were sea horses and starfish, schools of fish that numbered in the thousands, and even sharks and whales. And it wasn't like Lagoona was by herself. In addition to her mom and dad, she had two little sisters and a school of brothers. But there were no other monsters in the Great Barrier Reef who were her age—and that was what really made her feel all alone, even when surrounded by thousands of other sea creatures.

For the first time in her life, though, Lagoona had an unshakable feeling that all that was about to change. She would never forget the thrill of hope that had unfurled in her heart when she first read Draculaura's message about the new monsters-only school she was starting. In fact,

Lagoona had shrieked so loudly that both her parents had come swimming, terrified that an adventurous Normie had scu-boo-dived right into their secret undersea home. At first, her parents hadn't understood why she was so excited to live and study at Monster High. They didn't understand why she wasn't every bit as happy as they were in their spacious sea home. Somehow, though, Lagoona had managed to convince them that she needed to go to Monster High. Now all she had to do was wait for a response from Draculaura.

When Lagoona finally surfaced, she realized that she'd missed the sunrise entirely: A heavy bank of clouds had blown in on a stiff wind while she was underwater. The waves were already choppier than before, with foamy whitecaps like warning flags. She hoped that the Normies on the beach would notice her signs. Scanning the horizon, Lagoona realized that there weren't any sailboats or cruise ships as far as she could see. Even the fishing boats knew better than to risk being out in a tropical cyclone, which meant one very important thing to Lagoona: It was time to grab her surfboard!

Lagoona dove back under the waves and swam around the coral reef until she reached the grotto's entrance, which was almost undetectable unless you knew where to look. Her little sisters, Kelpie and Ebbie, were at the computer. Lagoona's heart skipped.

"Any news?" she asked. "Did Draculaura respond to my message?"

"No," Kelpie said. "And g'day to you too."

Lagoona tried to squelch her disappointment. "Oh. How come you two are hovering around my computer?" she asked.

"We were waiting for you," Ebbie replied. "You're always checking for new messages on your computer, so we figured this was the best place to find you."

Lagoona smiled sheepishly. It was true that she had become a little bit obsessed with checking for new messages on the Monster Web—no, make that a *lot* obsessed. She couldn't help herself! After all, Draculaura's response could come at any moment...though in her heart, Lagoona was starting to worry. Several days had passed, yet there was still no word from Draculaura—or from anyone else at Monster High. How much longer would she have to wait?

Kelpie's voice interrupted Lagoona's thoughts. "Everybody else is surfing already. Did you see the sky?" she asked with a mischievous smile.

"Did I ever," Lagoona replied. "Go on, grab your boards. If this is just a short squall, we don't want to miss another moment."

"Dad doesn't think it's a squall at all," Ebbie told her. "He thinks a cyclone's coming!"

"Fintastic!" Lagoona replied. "That means we can have an even longer surf sesh than usual."

Lagoona grabbed her board and was about to follow her sisters into the waves when she glanced at her computer again. *Won't hurt to check it once more*, she thought to herself. Just approaching the computer made her heart quicken. But when she refreshed, her Monster Web mailbox was still empty. Lagoona hadn't really expected that a message from Draculaura would've arrived in the last thirty seconds...but then again...

What if something's wrong with my Monster Web connection? Lagoona thought suddenly. It was tricky to get a connection this deep underwater, and it wouldn't be the first time a looming storm had caused the circuits to go haywire. Lagoona decided to adjust her settings and run a systems check to see.

Maybe I'll send another message to Draculaura,

Lagoona thought. She didn't want to seem super needy, but if something had gone wrong and Draculaura hadn't received her first message...

Lagoona's fins brushed against the keyboard as she started to type.

> G'day, Draculaura! Just a quick hi before I head out for a surf session with my sibs. Really excited about Monster High still! Can't wait to hear from you! xo Lagoona

"Lagoona!" Ebbie's voice carried through the water. "Come on! We're missing all the fun!"

"I'm on my way," Lagoona called back. The system scan would take a couple of hours, and she didn't want to disappoint her sisters. It was scary-sweet of them to wait for her before they hit the waves. As Lagoona swam to the surface with her board tucked under her arm, she found that she was even more excited about surfing through the squall.

After all, Lagoona had a feeling that she needed to get in as many surf sessions as she could—before it was time to move to Monster High!

CHAPTER 3

Let's start by listening to Lagoona's message again," Draculaura suggested. Everyone gathered around her iCoffin while she played it.

"Draculaura! Ghoulfriend!" a voice with an accent said. "This is Lagoona from Down Unda! I'm ready to dry off my scales for a while and start a new adventure with some fintastic ghoulfriends! Can you help me get to Monster High? Thanks, mate!"

"Down Unda?" Frankie said. "That could be a nickname for the Great Barrier Reef, near Australia."

"Clawesome clue!" Clawdeen cheered. "Hey, what about 'dry off my scales'? Could Lagoona be a sea monster?"

"Maybe," Draculaura replied. "It doesn't really matter, though. Monster High welcomes *all* monsters—no matter how scaly they are!"

Suddenly, Draculaura's iCoffin beeped to alert her to a new message. "It's from Lagoona!" she exclaimed. Then she read the message aloud. *"G'day, Draculaura! Just a quick hi before I head out for a surf session with my sibs. Really excited about Monster High still! Can't wait to hear from you! xo Lagoona."*

Draculaura could tell how excited Lagoona was to come to Monster High. Draculaura couldn't wait to bring her to the school, and she typed out a quick response to let Lagoona know that the ghouls were on their way! But as she hit SEND, something occurred to her.

"We didn't make plans for surfing at Monster High," Draculaura said. She sounded a little worried. "Do you think Lagoona will be upset about that? What if it's her favorite hobby?"

"Well, even if it is her favorite hobby—" started Clawdeen.

"All we have is a pool and the lake, but it sounds like she might be a saltwater ghoul," Draculaura thought aloud. "Maybe we should look into digging a new body of water and making it salty so Lagoona will feel right at home!" Draculaura said excitedly. She grinned, showcasing her impressive fangs. "Or maybe Frankie can build a wave machine so that Lagoona can still surf. Oh, we can draw up the plans right now! If we just take this acre over here—"

"I heard that, and we will absolutely not be building a mini-ocean in the backyard!" called Dracula from down the hall.

"Ha-ha, well, maybe not a whole ocean..." Draculaura said to her friends, blushing. "I just want to make sure Lagoona loves it here!"

"Ghoul, she is going to *love* Monster High," Clawdeen said firmly. "Don't start worrying about stuff you can't control. Besides, she'll probably pick up a bunch of new hobbies here."

"Or join some clubs!" Frankie suggested. Then she paused. "Wait a second. Do we even have clubs?"

"Not yet, but I'm sure we'll have a ton of extra-curricular activities," Draculaura replied. "We could have Casketball or fearleading—"

Cleo drummed her fingers impatiently on the table. "Focus, ghouls," she ordered. "Like I said before, Lagoona is *dying* to get here. So—how are we gonna make it happen?"

"So here's a crazy idea," Frankie spoke up.

All the ghouls turned to her.

"What if we just...go?" she asked.

"Fang on a minute! Wasn't doing our research the whole point of coming back? That, and to get some Mummy Mocha refills," Clawdeen said as she took a big gulp of her drink.

"You're right," Frankie explained. "But this is more like a quick trip as *part* of our research."

"I get it!" Draculaura exclaimed. "It wouldn't be a full-fledged rescue mission. Not yet, anyway. I think it's a great idea!"

"And the rest of us can stay here to start some research. I'd go, but I'm a little worried about the water," Frankie explained. "Sometimes I get a little—sparky—if I'm not careful. And I do *not* feel like short-circuiting today. So, does anyone want to volunteer?"

"Me!" Draculaura and Clawdeen exclaimed at the same time.

"I'm just fine here!" quipped Cleo.

"Voltageous!" Frankie cheered. "There's safety in numbers, after all."

Just then, Dracula appeared in the doorway. "Did someone say, 'safety'?" he asked.

Here we go, Draculaura thought. "Dad, were you eavesdropping again?" she asked, pretending to scold him.

"Of course not!" Dracula replied. "But I do have to ask—what are you ghouls up to?"

"We're working on a plan to bring Monster High's next student to campus," Draculaura explained. "Her name is Lagoona Blue. Clawdeen and I are going to use the Monster Mapalogue to learn a little more about where she lives. All we know so far is that it's pretty watery."

"Watery!" Dracula exclaimed. "Sit tight. I know just what you need!"

"Uh-oh," Draculaura whispered to her ghoul-friends. "I feel like I should apologize in advance for whatever embarrassing thing my dad is about to do."

"Aw, he's just being a dad," Frankie said. "Don't be embarrassed!"

"Life vests!" Dracula's voice rang through the Creepeteria.

"*Err*, never mind," whispered Frankie. "That's definitely embarrassing!"

Draculaura cringed at the sight of the bright-orange vests, which gleamed with stripes of shiny reflective tape. "Dad! Those are totes gross!" She groaned. "Why would Lagoona want to come to Monster High with a pair of floating pumpkins?"

"On the contrary, she'll probably be *very* impressed with how safety conscious you are!" Dracula replied.

"Seriously, Mr. D.—I don't need it," Clawdeen said, holding up her hands. "I was born knowing how to doggy-paddle."

"I don't doubt that for a minute," Dracula replied. "Still, if you're going to be in the water,

I must insist. Now, I've got four life vests here—one for each of you."

"That's okay," Cleo replied. "Only Clawdeen and Draculaura are going this time."

"Oh, perfect—then you can each wear *two* life vests!" Dracula said brightly.

"No, that's okay," Draculaura said quickly. "One is enough. *More* than enough."

"And, of course, don't forget the sunscream. I have SPF 1000," Dracula continued. "Sun safety is just as important as water safety!"

"So—if we slather up and wear these lame vests—sorry, I mean *life* vests," Clawdeen began, "you'll let us go?"

There was a pause before Dracula answered.

"Yes," he said finally. "I don't love the thought of you ghouls bobbing around in an ocean far from home, but I know that you will be as careful as you can."

"Of course they will!" Frankie said. "Here, ghouls, let me help you get ready."

Cleo's gold earrings were so big and shiny that Draculaura and Clawdeen used them as mirrors, staring at their reflections as they rubbed the extra-thick sunscream over their skin. Then Dracula inflated the life vests.

"Um, I don't think it's possible to make these vests look good," Clawdeen whispered to Draculaura as the bulky life vests filled with air and got even bigger. "Are there any more fangtastic-looking options available?"

"Ghoul, I wish," Draculaura whispered back. "My dad has always been like this, but I think it's gotten a little worse since we started Monster High."

"Really?" asked Frankie.

Draculaura nodded. "Now it's not just me he worries about—but everybody else too!"

Dracula was breathless from blowing up the

life vests. "I—think—we're—just—about—done," he gasped.

Clawdeen raked back her thick hair and held it out of the way while Frankie and Cleo helped her put on the vest. "You know, maybe these life vests aren't the worst idea," she joked. "My mane is *not* easy to tame if it gets tangled up from wind and salt water."

"I guess we'll know soon enough," Draculaura replied as she fastened her buckles. *Click. Click. Click. Click.*

Clawdeen turned to Draculaura. "What do you think? Do I look ready?"

Draculaura stared at the puffy life vest and the goopy sunscream coating Clawdeen's cheeks. "Oh yeah," she said. "We look ready for *something*. What exactly, I'm not sure, but ready or not—let's go!"

Together, Draculaura and Clawdeen placed their fingertips on the Skullette. "Next stop,

Lagoona's home—wherever that is," Draculaura said. "*Lagoona. Exsto monstrum!*"

Whoosh!

The trip seemed faster than usual; Draculaura barely had a chance to breathe before she realized that she was falling. The plunge was swift and sudden; she felt the wetness of the water before she saw it. Draculaura braced herself, trying to take a deep breath before complete and total submersion. But thanks to the life vest, her head stayed above water, so she could breathe just fine.

"Clawdeen!" Draculaura cried as she bobbed like an apple on the sky-blue waters. "The life vests! They're keeping us afloat!"

"I could get used to this," Clawdeen replied as she drifted on the gentle waves.

"It's so relaxing," Draculaura agreed. "Too bad Cleo and Frankie didn't come too. They are definitely missing out!"

"Have you ever seen water this blue and clear?" Clawdeen asked. "It's fangtastic!"

Draculaura peered over the edge of her life vest. "Wow," she breathed. "I can see all the way down to the ocean floor. The sand is so white! It looks like pearls!"

"Check out those strands of seaweed—they're like ribbons," added Clawdeen.

"Do you think there are any coral reefs near here?" Draculaura asked as she glanced around.

"Maybe," Clawdeen said. "Actually, we must be pretty far out. I don't see anything—not the beach, not an island, nothing."

"The water must be even deeper than it looks," said Draculaura. "We *have* to remember all this. It will definitely help us figure out exactly where we are."

"Oh, I know where we are," Clawdeen joked, leaning back as far as her life vest would let her.

"Paradise! I would love to take a scarecation here someday."

"Maybe Lagoona really is a sea monster and lives out here!" Draculaura said excitedly. "I can't *wait* to meet her."

"You know who else can't wait?" asked Clawdeen. "That school of fish over there. Look how fast they're swimming!"

"Slow down, little fishies," Draculaura joked.

"Yeah, what's the hurry? You should relax, like us," Clawdeen said. "Right, Drac?"

But Draculaura didn't answer.

"Right, Drac?" Clawdeen repeated. She reached out and gave Draculaura's shoulder a little shake. "You okay? You look really pale all of a sudden. Or maybe it's just the sunscream."

"It's not the sunscream," Draculaura said, her voice barely more than a whisper. "Ghoul, look over there. Are you seeing what I'm seeing?"

Clawdeen shielded her eyes with her hand as she peered at the horizon. The brilliant sun shone so brightly that the water around them sparkled, which made it hard to see. Clawdeen squinted—strained her eyes—and then she finally realized why Draculaura was so pale.

"Is that a *shark fin?*" Clawdeen cried.

"I think so," Draculaura replied. "No wonder those fish were swimming so fast! We'd better get out of here too."

"Let's try not to make any sudden motions," Clawdeen said. "Maybe it won't see us."

"Maybe," Draculaura said. "But I think it noticed us long before we noticed it."

Clawdeen swallowed hard. "I have a funny feeling about this."

"Me too," Drac replied. "Don't look now—but I think it's coming this way!"

CHAPTER 4

Lagoona lay down on her board and paddled farther out to sea. The approaching wave was big—bigger than any other wave she'd caught that morning. When it began to crest, she wanted to be ready, in just the right position to ride it all the way home. And she would be. After all, Lagoona had been surfing ever since she'd learned to swim as a baby.

A new sound arose over the steady lapping of the water as the tides formed a tall, white-capped wave. Lagoona pulled herself into a crouching position. Then, carefully steadying herself, she started to stand.

"You ready, Ebbie? Kelpie?" Lagoona called to her sisters. "Watch and learn!"

"Go, Lagoona!" her sisters cried. "Hang ten!"

"Three...two...*one!*" Lagoona screamed as the wave met her board and catapulted her over the churning waters at top speed. The wind blew her hair into a wild tangle, but Lagoona didn't care. The only thing she felt was a sense of joy that swelled as large as the wave, filling her with exhilaration.

Over the roar of the waves, Lagoona could hear her sisters cheering as she showed off her best moves, peaking when she managed to pull off an aerial without wiping out. She couldn't stop grinning as she maneuvered over to Ebbie and Kelpie.

"Good on ya, Lagoona!" Kelpie said as they all swam toward home. "Do you think I'll ever surf as well as you?"

"Do I think it? No," Lagoona teased. "I *know* it!"

"But how will I ever learn after you go off to Monster High?" Kelpie replied.

Lagoona gave her sister a hug. "Of course you'll learn," she said. "Besides, I'll come home whenever we have scaremester breaks. You can't get rid of me that easily!"

"We're still going to miss you," Ebbie said with a pout.

"Then I guess I'll have to call you lots to make up for it," Lagoona told her sisters as they reached their hidden grotto. When they were all smiles again, she slipped away to check her computer for a message from Draculaura. She hoped the systems check was complete and everything would be up and running again.

But when Lagoona got to her computer, the screen was black. She didn't even have a weak connection to the Monster Web anymore!

What is it this time? Lagoona wondered. *Corroded cables? Waterlogged wires?*

"Mum!" Lagoona called. "Help! The Monster Web is dead!"

"Again?" Lagoona's mother asked as she swam over to her.

"Look at the router—no signal," Lagoona told her. "This is dreadful! What if Draculaura's trying to message me *right now?*"

"Don't fuss, it will probably just end up in the queue. You'll get it when we fix the connection," Mum said. "But that might be a while. Your dad and I saw a pair of Normies in the deep water, bobbing around in those silly inflatable vests they like to wear. They're gone now, but he wants to keep watch in case they come back. It's unusual for them to be this far out."

"Normies?" Lagoona was instantly alert. "With the tropical cyclone coming? But I posted so many warning signs this morning!"

Mum smiled affectionately. "You and your Dawn Patrol," she said. "But Normies have a mind of their own, dearie. You know that."

"But—" Lagoona began.

"I've got to fix some brekkie for the little ones," Mum continued. "Don't worry about Draculaura. I'm sure you'll be hearing from her soon."

Lagoona was still troubled, even after Mum left the room. *Why would a couple of Normies ignore my signs and go so far out in these conditions?* she wondered. *It doesn't make sense.*

She flipped the switch on the router back and forth, but it never lit up. That told Lagoona that the problem wasn't with her computer. From the look of things, the whole Monster Web was down in this section of the ocean.

Lagoona sat there, deep in thought. Then she

abruptly stood up and swam toward the grotto's hidden entrance.

I'll go find Dad, she decided. *Maybe he can help me fix the connection. And if those Normies come back...I want to see them for myself!*

CHAPTER 5

"Ghoul, we've gotta go!" Clawdeen shrieked as the shark approached.

Draculaura was already on it. She thrust the Skullette toward Clawdeen; the instant Clawdeen touched it, Draculaura uttered, *"Monster High. Exsto monstrum!"*

Whoosh!

The ghouls, sopping wet and a little dizzy, found themselves sprawled on the floor of the

Creepeteria. They were covered in big chunks of seaweed from the ocean. Dracula took one look at them and hurried away to get some towels while Frankie and Cleo rushed to their sides.

"You're soaked!" Frankie cried, making sure to keep a safe distance from the pool of seawater that was spreading across the Creepeteria floor. "And kind of gross. What happened out there? A seaweed storm?"

"Seaweed wraps are all the rage, you know," said Cleo as she happily helped her ghoulfriends to their feet.

"Oh my ghoul, you will not even believe what happened," Draculaura began. "The Monster Mapalogue dropped us in *shark-infested* waters!"

Frankie and Cleo gasped in unison. Then Cleo gave a quizzical look. "Um, what are 'sharks'?" she asked.

"Predatory sea creatures with literally hundreds of sharp, pointy teeth!" answered Frankie.

"More like *thousands*," Clawdeen corrected her. "The shark was coming straight at us too!"

Draculaura shivered. "Like it had just spotted its next meal."

Cleo gave Drac a big hug and didn't even flinch when Draculaura dripped seawater all over her teal-and-gold tunic. "Not on my watch," she promised. "I will not permit some slimy, smelly shark to menace *my* best ghoulfriends."

Draculaura flashed her a grateful smile. "Thanks, Cleo," she replied. "I hate to admit it, but maybe Dad was right about the life vests...and how dangerous it is out there...and everything else too."

"I heard that!" Dracula said as he entered the room with a stack of thick, fluffy towels. "And you're welcome."

"I'm so glad that Drac and Clawdeen were brave enough for the recon mission," Frankie said. "If I'd been plunged into salt water like that..."

Frankie's voice trailed off.

"What?" Cleo whispered, her eyes wide.

"Short-circuit central," Frankie said. She pointed at the bolts on either side of her neck. "As you know, water and electricity definitely do *not* mix. Plus, salt water is corrosive. It could eat through my bolts in no time—which would be a huge disaster."

Clawdeen let out a low whistle. "Does that mean...you can't help us rescue Lagoona?"

Draculaura held her breath. Clawdeen had said what they were all thinking, but Draculaura wasn't sure she was ready for the answer.

"I don't know..." Frankie replied thoughtfully. "I can tell you this, though—I won't go on the mission if there's even a chance I could put you ghouls in danger. Hopefully it's just a piece of the puzzle we haven't solved yet."

"There are a *lot* of pieces to this puzzle," Cleo grumbled. "Corrosive water—ghoul-eating sharks—and a demented Mapalogue that throws us right into the middle of them. Can we get a do-over?"

Draculaura shook her head. "I don't think it works like that," she said. "I don't know exactly how the Monster Mapalogue decides where to send us, but I have a feeling it takes us right where we need to go—whether we know it or not."

"True," Frankie agreed. "I mean, we *thought* we were in the middle of an empty desert when we set off to rescue you, Cleo—but it turned out we were really close to your tomb."

"We just didn't know it at the time," added Clawdeen.

"So that gets us back to what we were talking about earlier," Draculaura said. "All the things we *don't* know about how to rescue Lagoona. Like how to get Frankie there safely."

"And avoid being eaten by a giant shark," said Clawdeen.

"And maybe *not* get dunked in the middle of some faraway ocean?" Cleo said hopefully. "I mean, as much as I'd love a free organic seaweed wrap, the ocean doesn't sound like my thing."

"Ghouls, we can do this," Draculaura said with a rush of confidence. She flung her arms out wide. "I mean, look at this! We have *all* of Monster High available to us! We can learn anything here!"

"Which means we can do anything out there," Frankie said, pointing at the window.

"I still haven't heard back from Lagoona," Draculaura said as she reached for her phone. "I'm going to send her a message to check in."

Drac's pale fingers flew across the screen as she tapped each letter.

Hey, ghoul! It's Drac. I took a quick trip to your area—did you see me? Not sure exactly where I was—we were surrounded by water and there were giant sharks (eek!). Any ideas?

The other ghouls and I will be back as soon
as we figure out how to reach you. xo Drac

Draculaura hit SEND and was about to ask
her ghoulfriends a question when her phone
beeped. "Lagoona wrote back!" she shrieked. The
ghouls crowded around excitedly—but the message Draculaura had received was not what they
expected.

MESSAGE UNDELIVERABLE
Your message was not received by the
intended monster.

"Oh. Guess I was wrong," Draculaura said,
frowning at the screen.

"Did you get that message when you reached
out to Lagoona earlier?" asked Cleo.

"No, I didn't," replied Draculaura. "Which
means…"

"Her connection to the Monster Web has gone out," Frankie finished for her. "I bet that happens all the time where she lives. All that salt water... high winds and waves..."

"Poor ghoul," Cleo said. "I would've been *lost* without the Monster Web while I was stuck in my tomb for a whole millennia!"

"We don't have even a minute to lose," announced Draculaura. "Come on, ghouls! Let's go get Lagoona!"

"Next stop—the library!" Frankie cheered.

"So, we've got three problems," Draculaura began as the ghouls climbed the spiral staircase to the second floor. "Number one: We don't know very much about the Great Barrier Reef."

"True," Cleo replied.

"Number two: We have a big—and I mean *big*—shark problem," Draculaura continued.

"*Very* true," Clawdeen said as she made a face.

"And number three: We have a ghoulfriend who really shouldn't touch the water," Draculaura finished, glancing at Frankie.

"Too true, I'm afraid," Frankie said with a sigh.

"Anything else?" asked Drac.

"I—" Cleo began.

Everyone turned to look at her.

Cleo paused, smiled brightly, and shrugged. "I don't think so," she said.

But as Cleo looked away, Draculaura noticed there was something a little, well, *off* about her eyes. Was she annoyed? Or maybe worried? Draculaura couldn't quite figure it out. *This must be so overwhelming*, Draculaura thought. Just hours ago, Cleo was trapped in her tomb. And now she was out in the monster world, about to set off on her first rescue mission. Total culture shock!

"How about we start with researching the Great Barrier Reef?" Frankie's voice jolted Draculaura out of her thoughts.

"Definitely," Draculaura replied. "We just need to find the right book!"

Monster High's library was enormous, filled with thousands of books about monster history, monster lore, and more. The ghouls split up, drifting throughout the library as they searched for books that would help them. After Draculaura found a book called *The Wundas of Down Unda: The Great Barrier Reef and Beyond*, she noticed Cleo all alone in the corner—and that gave her an idea.

Draculaura crossed the room to Clawdeen. "*Psst!* Clawdeen!" she whispered.

"What's up?" Clawdeen whispered back as she glanced up from her book.

"I'm a little worried about Cleo," Draculaura replied. "She seems—I don't know. Like maybe she feels out of place."

"That's not good," Clawdeen said right away. "She's one of us now! Monster High should feel like home."

"That's what I think," Draculaura said. "But it is a big change for her."

"Totally," Clawdeen agreed. "What should we do?"

"I was just thinking, maybe she'd feel more at home if we tried really, really hard to be the best ghoulfriends ever," Draculaura said.

"You got it," Clawdeen replied.

Just then, Frankie's voice rang through the library. "Ghouls! I found an atlas!" she called.

Clawdeen, Draculaura, and Cleo hurried over to her. Frankie lugged the heavy book off the shelf and dropped it on a long wooden table. A cloud of dust rose into the air, sparkling as it caught the light. Draculaura's nose tickled, but little Webby, Drac's pet spider, sneezed so hard he flew halfway across the room.

"Sorry, Webby," Clawdeen called over her shoulder.

Draculaura leaned over the enormous book

and began to turn its yellowed pages. "This is scary-cool," she said. "It looks like there are maps of the entire world here."

"Maybe even a map of where Monster High is located!" Frankie said.

"Check this out!" Draculaura exclaimed. "This map is of the...ocean?"

The ghouls leaned over the page to get a closer look. Brilliant swirls of crystal-clear water hid—*almost* hid—an intricate design that looked like a craggy, crooked structure.

"What *is* that?" asked Cleo.

"If I'm not mistaken, that's the Great Barrier Reef," Frankie told her.

"It's totally underwater?" Cleo said, sounding surprised. "I mean—*all* of it?"

"Well, not exactly," Frankie replied. "There are lots of small islands in the Great Barrier Reef. But the reef itself is made of coral, so it's all underwater. Listen to this," she said before reading aloud.

"The coral structures of the Great Barrier Reef provide an ecosystem for thousands of types of sea creatures. There are more than a hundred islands in the system."

"And, apparently, sea monsters," Draculaura said, thinking of Lagoona.

"It makes sense, doesn't it?" asked Clawdeen. "Those coral structures could provide a ton of hiding places for a monster who wanted to avoid Normies."

"But couldn't Lagoona be on one of the islands too?" Cleo asked hopefully. "More than a hundred islands—that's a lot! I bet a monster could definitely hide out there!"

"Maybe," Draculaura said. "But the Monster Mapalogue sent us straight into the sea. That's probably a sign."

Cleo's face fell. "Oh. Right," she said. "I forgot about that."

"So it sounds like we'd better be ready for a watery trip," Frankie said with a worried frown.

"Hey," Draculaura said. "The most important thing is for you to stay safe. I don't want you getting dunked in the deep if it's going to make you short out."

"I don't want that, either," Frankie said. "But I'm not ready to give up. Not yet!"

"Of course not," Clawdeen said firmly. "Who said anything about giving up? In fact..."

As Clawdeen's voice trailed off, her eyes lit up. "Clawesome!" she exclaimed.

"What?" Frankie, Draculaura, and Cleo said—all at the same time.

But Clawdeen just smiled mysteriously. "You'll see," she said. Then she reached out and grabbed Cleo's hand. "Come on. I'm going to need your help."

Then, without another word, Clawdeen and Cleo ran out of the library.

Draculaura and Frankie exchanged a look of

surprise. "What was *that* about?" Frankie finally asked.

"I have no idea—but I can't wait to find out what Clawdeen's big idea is," said Draculaura.

"Me too," Frankie agreed. "And I've had a big idea of my own."

"Tell me everything!" Draculaura exclaimed.

"We don't need to worry about the water just for *my* sake," Frankie began. "We need to worry about it for all of us. I don't think the life vests are enough."

"Go on," Draculaura encouraged her.

"Scu-boo gear!" Frankie exclaimed. "A combination mask and breathing apparatus so we can explore the ocean floor if we need to."

"That's fangtastic!" replied Draculaura. "Any chance you can make it shark-repellent too?" she added with a hopeful grin. "You know, like bug repellent but for sharks?"

"I can try." Frankie laughed. "But I don't think we can make bug spray for sharks. Either way, I'd better get to the lab."

"I'll come too," Draculaura offered. She tucked *The Wundas of Down Unda: The Great Barrier Reef and Beyond* under her arm.

The Mad Science lab at Monster High was Frankie's favorite place in the whole school. Tucked in the deepest underground basement, it was surprisingly high-tech—just the way Frankie liked it. The steel countertops, chrome cabinets, and ultra-bright lights reminded her of the power station where she'd grown up. Best of all, though, the Mad Science lab was fully stocked with everything an inventor could possibly need—from chemical compounds and rare earth elements to beakers and Bunsen burners.

The ghouls were quiet as Frankie assembled everything she needed to start work on the scu-boo gear: tubes and valves, heavy-duty sheets of plastic, and some unusual iridescent tanks that caught Draculaura's eye. "What are those?" she asked.

Frankie didn't look up as she started adjusting the valves on the tanks. "It's a new oxygen containment system," she explained. "It doesn't even have a name yet. But if my theory is correct…"

"What?" asked Draculaura.

Frankie flashed her a quick grin. "I don't want to jinx it," she replied. "Let's just wait and see if it works!"

For a while, the only sound in the lab was Frankie as she made the deep-sea scu-boo gear. At last, she broke the silence by asking Draculaura, "What are you learning about sea creatures?"

"Tons of cool stuff!" Drac replied. "I mean, the Great Barrier Reef is literally packed with sea creatures of all kinds…and *that's* what attracts predators like the shark I saw. So it probably was looking for its next meal!"

Draculaura shuddered at the thought.

"But the good news is that sharks generally don't want to eat monsters—or even Normies," she continued. "They prefer smaller fish or crustaceans, something they can chomp in one bite. And they usually attack only when they're feeling confused or threatened."

"Interesting," Frankie replied. "So we should be okay, unless the shark gets scared of *us?*"

"I think the best advice is to steer clear of them," Draculaura told her. "But that might be easier said than done. We can't exactly control where sharks swim, you know?"

"True!" Frankie laughed. "You know what else we can't control? The weather."

"It was like a paradise when Clawdeen and I were there," Draculaura told Frankie. "Clear blue skies…clear blue seas…and a brilliant, glittering sun."

"So we will definitely need to be ready for the

heat," Frankie mused. "Do any of those books have a section on weather patterns in the Great Barrier Reef? We could read up so we know what kind of weather to expect."

Draculaura flipped to the index. "This one does," she replied. "But honestly, there wasn't a single cloud in the sky."

"Let's hope it stays that way," Frankie said. "But if it doesn't—we'll be ready!"

CHAPTER 6

Meanwhile, Clawdeen and Cleo were hard at work in Monster High's art studio. The large, airy room was monstrously bright, which made it the perfect place for all sorts of artistic endeavors, from painting to pottery. Clawdeen had always loved to paint, and her scaritage included lots of artists. In fact, her own mother was Monster High's art teacher. But painting wasn't the reason why Clawdeen had brought Cleo to the art studio.

Cleo watched in confusion as Clawdeen

unfurled several bolts of fabric, shaking her head in disappointment before tossing each one back in a pile.

"Ghoul, what could you be looking for?" Cleo finally asked. "The royal seamstress never worked this hard, and I have *very* particular taste. All those fabrics look fangtastic to me."

Clawdeen glanced up for a moment. "Oh, they are," she assured Cleo. "For, you know, outfits. It's just—I have something different in mind."

"Tell me more!" Cleo said excitedly. "Starting new trends happens to be a talent of mine. Maybe I can help!"

"I want to design a special suit for Frankie," Clawdeen explained. "Something completely waterproof—so she can help find Lagoona without worrying about going all sparky."

"That would be golden," Cleo replied.

"But it's not enough for it to be waterproof," Clawdeen continued. "It has to be positively clawesome too. I do *not* want poor Frankie stuck in the equivalent of a full-body life vest."

They both shuddered at the thought.

"What can I do to help?" asked Cleo.

Clawdeen crossed the room, rummaged through one of the cabinets, and returned with a sketchbook and a set of freshly sharpened colored pencils. "Do you want to help me sketch some designs?" she asked. "I'll have my hands full trying to find the right materials and making the patterns. Plus, your style is totally clawesome. If you bring just a smidgen of that style to Frankie's suit, she can look voltageous and stay safe at the same time."

"I'm just the ghoul for the job!" Cleo replied with a smile.

Cleo started sketching while Clawdeen returned to the pile of fabrics. After a while, Clawdeen exclaimed "Yes!" so loud that Cleo jumped.

"I found it!" Clawdeen cried. She held up a bolt

of silvery material that shimmered whenever it caught the light.

"It's golden," Cleo said approvingly. "But is it waterproof?"

"One hundred percent guaranteed," Clawdeen said, pointing at the label on the end of the bolt. "But I think we can do even better than that."

"Let me guess," Cleo replied. "Double layers?"

"Exactly," Clawdeen said. "Plus, I was thinking of crossing the two layers of fabric to make them even stronger."

"It will have to be head to toe," Cleo reminded her. She pushed the sketchbook across the table to Clawdeen. "What do you think of my design?"

Clawdeen leaned over to study Cleo's sketch. The sleek suit had a futuristic feel that would fit Frankie's high-tech personality perfectly. "*Ooh, that's clawesome!*" Clawdeen said approvingly when she noticed the small, stiff fins that Cleo had added to the suit's arms and back.

"If they're good enough for these 'sharks' you speak of, I figured they'll be good for Frankie's suit," Cleo said with a laugh. "And if we coat the thread with wax before we sew the suit, even the thread will be waterproof. That will make the seams even stronger—and make sure that Frankie stays dry."

"Ghoul, you're a genius!" Clawdeen exclaimed. "Why didn't I think of that?"

"Well, you know, my tomb was accidentally sealed with beeswax for, like, a thousand years," Cleo said. "I had a lot of time to think about stuff like that."

"But we *don't* have a lot of time before we need to get to Lagoona," Clawdeen reminded her. "Do you know how to sew?"

Cleo blinked. "Sew?" she repeated. "Like... with a needle and thread?"

"Yeah," Clawdeen said. "That's usually how it's done."

"I wouldn't know," Cleo replied. "My seamstress

always did a marvelous job, though. Oh, if she were here we'd be done in no time! Maybe we could make a call…"

"Oh. Right," Clawdeen replied. "Well, I'll just get to work on the sewing, and—"

"Or maybe I could learn?" Cleo suggested a little shyly.

Clawdeen grinned at her ghoulfriend. "I think you could *definitely* learn," she replied. "Let's do it!"

For the next hour, Clawdeen taught Cleo everything she knew about creating a new fashion design—cutting out a pattern, tracing it onto fabric, pinning the pieces, and finally sewing the pieces together. Then came the fun part— embellishments! Cleo used a smooth, golden disc of beeswax to coat multicolor metallic thread, which the ghouls used to stitch half circles on every inch of the wetsuit. They glimmered and gleamed like fish scales—and provided even more protection from the water.

At last, Clawdeen held up the suit. "Ta-da!" she announced. "What do you think?"

"It's royal!" Cleo exclaimed. "Frankie is going to love it! Come on, let's go give it to her. I can't wait to see her face!"

"Uh-uh," Clawdeen replied, shaking her head. "It's not finished yet."

Cleo looked surprised. "What do you mean?" she asked. "It's got three layers of waterproofing; it's got functional *and* fashionable fins; it's even got some creepy-cool patterns. What else could we possibly do?"

"A trial run!" Clawdeen announced. She held out the suit to Cleo.

"Me?" Cleo asked in surprise. "You want *me* to try it on?"

"Not just try it on—swim in it!" Clawdeen told her.

Cleo stared at her with a blank look.

"Well, I would, but there's no way the hood will fit over my hair," Clawdeen explained, shaking her thick purple-streaked hair away from her face. "And there's no way we can give it to Frankie if we haven't tested it yet. That would be way too big a risk. Luckily, Monster High has a pool where we can test it out. Follow me!"

Clawdeen was so excited to see if the wetsuit worked that she didn't notice that Cleo was strangely quiet on their walk to Monster High's pool. The aqua-colored water in the pool rippled slightly, casting a flickering reflection on the purple and gray arches that lined the walls.

Clawdeen leaned over and dipped in her pinkie finger. "*Ahhh*, the water feels great!" she said. "I'm jealous. I'd love to take a dip!"

"Yeah! The pool looks great with all that water and the...uh, water..." Cleo echoed. She tried to smile but couldn't quite manage it.

"The locker room is over there," Clawdeen said. "Go ahead and get changed. Then you can test out the wetsuit."

"Maybe we should get Draculaura to test it," Cleo suggested suddenly. "I get the sense *that* ghoul really loves fashion! She'd be a great model. I'm just, oh you know, not that…uh…into fashion?" Cleo finished. She raised her eyebrows hopefully, wondering if she'd been convincing.

"Ghoul, you love fashion. You tried to bring five golden trunks of custom-made clothing to Monster High! And this is *your* design," Clawdeen replied, raising her own eyebrows. "Plus, Drac's probably busy with her research. I don't think we should interrupt her."

"But—"

"Hurry up and get changed! I can't wait to see if it works!"

"Okay," Cleo said slowly. Then she started walking toward the locker room. She moved as if her feet were encased in cement blocks instead of creeperific sandals.

Several minutes later, Cleo finally reappeared, wearing the wetsuit. The light reflecting off the saltwater pool made her look like a rare tropical sea beastie as it flickered off the shimmery threads.

Clawdeen nodded approvingly. "Well, the suit looks ugh-mazing," she said. "Now let's see if it really works."

"So...you just want me to, like, jump in?" Cleo asked doubtfully.

"Sure," Clawdeen said. "Go ahead! The water feels great!"

Cleo slowly inched closer to the edge of the pool. "Maybe I could just put my foot in?" she suggested. "That will tell us if the fabric really is waterproof."

But Clawdeen shook her head. "That will only tell us if it's waterproof on your foot," she replied. "What about the rest of Frankie's wetsuit? No, I think you've got to go underwater. You need to be *completely* submerged."

"Completely?" Cleo gulped.

"From head to toe," Clawdeen replied.

"Okay," Cleo said. She took a deep breath and let the tips of her toes hang over the edge of the pool. She lifted her foot, then started to lower it into the water. Slowly…slowly…*slowly*…

"I can't!" Cleo suddenly cried. She rushed backward from the pool and perched on the edge of a bench, hugging her knees tightly against her chest.

"Ghoul! What's wrong?" Clawdeen asked as she hurried to Cleo's side.

"I can't swim!" Cleo cried. Then she buried her face in her hands.

Clawdeen's mouth dropped open in shock. "Why didn't you say anything?" she asked.

"I—I—I was embarrassed," Cleo replied, her voice muffled. "When everyone was making fun of the life vests earlier, it made me realize how ridiculous it is that I don't know how to swim."

"Oh no," Clawdeen replied. "I'm sorry, Cleo. We didn't mean to make you feel bad. Honestly, we had no idea that you can't swim!"

"I've lived in the middle of the desert for my entire life," Cleo told her. "It was all lounging on the pyramid sundeck, being fanned by palm leaves, and gazing at the dunes. Even if I had wanted to learn, there wasn't the opportunity."

"Well, there is now," Clawdeen declared.

There was a pause before Cleo lifted her head. Clawdeen could see her eyes looked shimmery, like they were filled with tears—or hope.

"I've already seen how fast you learn things," Clawdeen continued. "Look how quickly you figured out how to sew! That's harder than swimming!"

"It is?" Cleo replied.

"I think it is," Clawdeen said. "And you know

what? Monster High is pretty much *the* place to learn new things. Come on. I'll teach you how to swim myself."

"You—you will?" Cleo asked.

"Of course! Like I told Draculaura when we went to the Great Barrier Reef, I've been dog-paddling since I was a pup," Clawdeen said. She reached out and took hold of Cleo's hand, then pulled Cleo to her feet.

"Don't go anywhere," Clawdeen continued. "I'm going to get my swimsuit, and then we'll *both* take the plunge. You'll be swimming before you know it!"

CHAPTER 7

The four ghouls worked on their projects late into the night. The next morning, they were up bright and early—and ready for adventure!

"But first, a good breakfast," Dracula told the ghouls as he served them stacks of waffles with boo-berries and syrup. "I don't want you Mapaloguing all over the world on an empty stomach."

"Thanks, Dad," Draculaura said as she took a big bite.

"Are you sure you're all ready for your trip today?" Dracula asked with an edge of anxiety in his voice. "Is there anything else you need?"

"Don't worry about us, Mr. D.," Clawdeen replied confidently. "We aren't just prepared. We're *monstrously* prepared!" It was true. All the ghouls had packed waterproof bags with their canteens, snacks, and anything else they thought they might need on the trip.

But that wasn't all. Draculaura's eyes twinkled as she unzipped her bag. "Ready for a little show-and-tell?" she asked. "First up, Frankie!"

The bolts in Frankie's neck lit up as she showed everyone the scu-boo gear she'd built. "These masks are specially designed for deep waters. We might be under pressure, but we sure won't feel it!" she said. "And check out these oxygen tanks. They're filled with a super-condensed form of oxygen I pressurized in the lab. They barely weigh anything—but we'll be able to breathe for at least twenty hours underwater!"

"Ghoul, that is clawesome!" Clawdeen cheered. "Cleo and I were busy yesterday too. Check it out!"

With a big flourish, Clawdeen and Cleo presented Frankie with her new wetsuit. The look on Frankie's face shifted from confusion to astonishment to joy. "Is this what I think it is?" she squealed.

"Head to toe, fully waterproofed, and with reinforced waterproof seams!" Cleo announced. "Now you can come on the trip without worrying about short-circuiting!"

"This is so voltageous!" Frankie exclaimed. "How can I thank you?"

Clawdeen waved her hand in the air like it was no big deal. "No thanks necessary," she said. "It's just what ghoulfriends do for each other."

Cleo turned to Clawdeen. "Like teach them

how to sew *and* swim, all in one day," she said. "Ghoul, you are totally golden. I mean it."

A knowing smile crossed Clawdeen's face. "I have something for you too," she said. "I made this late last night. Hope you like it!"

Then Clawdeen surprised Cleo with a custom life vest—complete with gold scarab details that perfectly matched Cleo's outfit.

"You're a great swimmer for someone who has had only one day of lessons," Clawdeen continued. "But when you're going to swim in deep waters, well, you can't be too careful. What do you think?"

"I think..." Cleo began as a huge smile spread across her face, "I think I love it!"

"Ghoulfriend, you are so brave," Draculaura exclaimed. "One day of swimming lessons and you're ready to dive into the deep waters of the Great Barrier Reef. That is truly fangtastic!"

Cleo shrugged off the compliment, but everyone

could tell she was pleased. "What is there to be afraid of, when my best ghoulfriends have my back?" she asked. "Nothing!"

"Not even giant sharks?" teased Frankie.

"Just remember, they attack only when they feel anxious or scared. So if we see one, we'll just, uh, um—"

"Sing it a lullaby?" Clawdeen joked, making everyone laugh. "Teach it how to meditate?"

"If that's what it takes, then *yes!*" Draculaura continued.

"I'm going to put on my wetsuit," Frankie announced. "Be right back."

While they waited for Frankie, Clawdeen helped Cleo try on her new life vest, which fit perfectly. Then the other ghouls put on the scu-boo gear that Frankie had invented.

"This suit is spooktacular," Frankie announced when she rejoined the group. "Thank you so much!"

Draculaura looked at her ghoulfriends and marveled at how far they'd all come. Just days ago, they'd been struggling on their very first adventure in the harsh desert of Egypt, Cleo's homeland. And now they looked ready for anything that could happen on a deep-sea dive!

"So what do you think, ghouls? Are we ready, or are we *ready*?" Draculaura asked in excitement.

"Ready!" everyone cheered at the same time.

"Wait!" Dracula said.

The ghouls all turned to look at him.

"Don't forget extra sunscream!" he announced as he passed out four tubes, one for each ghoul.

"How could we ever forget that?" Draculaura said with a grin. She gave her dad a quick hug, then pulled out the Skullette. Her ghoulfriends reached over to place their fingers on it.

Draculaura took a deep breath. "*Lagoona... Exsto...monstrum!*" she said in a loud, clear voice.

Whoosh!

Draculaura was getting used to the way the Mapalogue transported her to a completely different location—well, *almost* used to it. Her fingers never left the Skullette; she thought she could feel her ghoulfriends holding on tightly too, and that made her feel a lot less alone—even though she couldn't see anything until—

Splash!

Splash!

Splash!

Splash!

One by one, the ghouls fell into the crystal-clear waters of the Great Barrier Reef.

Draculaura shut her eyes by instinct—but just as quickly, she realized that she didn't need to; Frankie's scu-boo mask would protect them from the stinging salt water. She opened her eyes just in time to see a million bubbles zipping up to the surface of the water. Draculaura used her hands to part them like a curtain, and, for the very first time, she saw the Great Barrier Reef up close. It was so astonishing that Draculaura could do nothing but stare in amazement.

Underwater, Draculaura could clearly see the exquisite coral structures: some that had ruffled edges, others that were lacy and delicate, and even more that protruded from the ocean floor like turrets on a castle. Thin blades of sea grass swayed back and forth from the ocean currents as thousands of fish in all colors darted through the reef. A large jellyfish, nearly translucent, whooshed through the water, trailing tentacles behind it like ribbons.

Draculaura could've stayed there watching the beautiful sea creatures for hours. Then, she remembered to look around for her ghoulfriends. She couldn't see them anywhere—but she had a feeling they weren't far away. Kicking her feet, Draculaura propelled herself to the surface of the water. Unlike her first trip to the Great Barrier

Reef, there was no dazzling sun to greet her. The gray clouds made the sky feel heavy, as if it were pressing down on her—but at least it was easier to see without the blinding sparkle of the sun on the water. She spotted Clawdeen, Cleo, and Frankie a few feet away and swam over to join them.

"Ghoul, what took you so long?" Clawdeen teased.

"It's truly fangtastic down there!" Draculaura exclaimed. "There are so many bright colors and funny little fishies. I've never seen anything like it!"

"The Great Barrier Reef is well known for its natural beauty," Frankie said. "That's why it's such a major tourist destination for Normies. We should keep an eye out for them, actually."

"Definitely," Clawdeen agreed. "I don't think we're *quite* ready for that."

"And I don't think they are, either," added Draculaura.

"Can you believe this ocean?" Cleo marveled. "I didn't even know there was this much water in the whole world!"

"It's so much bigger than I had imagined," added Frankie. "I mean, I knew it would be *massive*, but nothing could've prepared me."

"Seriously," Draculaura agreed. "I read an entire book on the Great Barrier Reef, and I'm still overwhelmed. Where do we even begin?"

The ghouls were quiet for a moment while they thought about it.

"Hey, I hate to bring up bad news," Frankie began as she pointed at the sky, "but did you ghouls notice that?"

Draculaura stared up. In the distance, the clouds looked darker—menacing, even.

"Those clouds weren't here yesterday," said Clawdeen. "We saw a couple of clouds, maybe, but nothing like this."

"They might not get any closer," Cleo suggested. "Not that I know anything about ocean
storms, obviously. But sometimes in the desert
we'd see faraway sandstorms, and they'd never
get anywhere near our tomb."

"Let's hope that happens for us," Frankie said.
"Because I do *not* like the look of those clouds. I
can feel—"

"What is it?" Draculaura asked when Frankie
stopped abruptly.

"It's probably nothing," Frankie answered. "But
sometimes my bolts get all tingly when there's
going to be an electrical storm. And you ghouls
do *not* want to be in the water if lightning strikes."

"We'd better move fast, then," Draculaura
replied. A damp breeze had kicked up; she
couldn't be completely sure, but it looked as if the
dark clouds were moving closer.

"Move where, exactly?" asked Cleo. "All I see is

water—no coastline, no islands, and not a single monster we could ask for help."

"No Normies, either," Clawdeen added.

Draculaura pointed into the depths of the water. "I was underwater over there," she said. "The reefs are amazing—and filled with sea creatures! Maybe Lagoona is down there with them. We are Down Unda, after all!"

"Let's take a look!" Frankie exclaimed as she paddled over to Draculaura.

"Ghouls, I'll stay at the surface," Cleo offered. "I can't dive underwater with my life vest, and this way I can keep an eye on that storm."

"Fangtastic idea," Draculaura told her. "You can signal to us if there's trouble—from storm or from shark."

"You got it," Cleo replied.

The ghouls adjusted their scu-boo masks and checked their oxygen tanks before they plunged underwater. Draculaura swam in the direction of the coral reef, while Clawdeen and Frankie followed close behind her. Soon, Drac saw the dramatic spires of coral twisting up from the sandy ocean floor. But there was a big difference from when she'd been underwater just minutes ago: Now there wasn't a single sea creature in sight.

That's weird, Draculaura thought. *Where did they all go? And...why?*

Then she recalled something she'd read in *The Wundas of Down Unda*. Coral reefs were especially popular with smaller sea creatures because they offered so many hidden, hard-to-see areas. *Maybe they didn't disappear*, Draculaura thought. *Maybe they're just hiding in plain sight.*

But unless a sea creature swam out to greet her, Draculaura didn't know how she'd find one. The coral reefs were as delicate as they were beautiful. She didn't dare risk damaging their fragile structures by swimming too close.

Just then, Draculaura felt a tap on her shoulder. She turned around to see Clawdeen and Frankie behind her. Even through their scu-boo masks, Draculaura could see the confused expressions on their faces. She shrugged to show them that she didn't know where all the fish and beasties had gone, either. Then Draculaura beckoned for the ghouls to follow as she swam to a different section of the reef.

This spot was eerily quiet too. The only motion came from the thin strands of sea grass that swayed back and forth with the currents.

This isn't right, Draculaura said. *The books all say that coral reefs are filled with life.*

A new worry started to gnaw at Draculaura. Had something happened to all the creatures who made their homes in the coral reefs? And if so—had it happened to Lagoona too?

Draculaura felt another tap on her shoulder. She turned around and saw Frankie pointing at the surface, and she understood perfectly.

It was time to regroup—and figure out what was going on.

CHAPTER 8

The first thing Draculaura heard when she popped her head above water was a scream.

It was Cleo!

She was waving wildly in the water, farther away than Draculaura remembered. *Either Cleo drifted away—or we did*, Draculaura thought as she started swimming as fast as she could.

Cleo screamed again.

Clawdeen was the fastest swimmer of all the ghouls. She blitzed past Frankie and Draculaura as she swam directly to Cleo, a blur zooming through the choppy water.

"What's wrong?" Clawdeen shouted to Cleo. Draculaura could just barely hear her voice, carried on the wind.

"I've been calling and calling for you ghouls!" Cleo cried, clearly upset. "Why did you swim so far?"

"Sorry," Draculaura apologized. "We didn't mean to. I think the current carried us away. The water's getting rougher."

Frankie put her arm around Cleo's shoulder and gave her a squeeze. "We would never leave you, ghoul!" she said.

"I know," Cleo said. "But that's not what I was worried about." She stretched out her arm and pointed at the horizon. "The shark is back!"

Draculaura's breath caught in her throat. She stared at the water. At first, she didn't see anything. "It's okay, ghouls," she began. "It's probably gone by now. Remember, sharks don't want to eat monsters. They—"

And then Draculaura saw it: a dark, sleek shape slicing through the water. The arced, pointed fin skimming through the waves told everyone that Cleo was right.

"Come on, ghouls!" Clawdeen said urgently. "We're about to be shark bait!"

"It's swimming right at us!" added Frankie.

Draculaura frowned. Something didn't seem quite right. "Wait a minute," she began.

"Drac! Let's go!" Frankie urged her.

Draculaura narrowed her eyes as she squinted, trying to get a better look.

"Draculaura! Please!" Cleo cried.

The creature was still swimming toward them. It came closer and closer until—

Draculaura spun around in the water to face her ghoulfriends. "It's not a shark!" she exclaimed in relief. "It's a dolphin!"

"Huh?" asked Cleo.

"How can you be so sure?" Frankie said.

"I read all about them in *The Wundas of Down Unda!*" Draculaura said excitedly. "See the fin? It would be much farther back on a shark. Plus, it would stand straight up—not curve backward."

"I've never seen a dolphin before," Clawdeen said. "Look at how it leaps over the waves!"

"Dolphins are playful creatures," Draculaura told the other ghouls. "But…"

"What?" asked Cleo.

"I'm not sure," Draculaura admitted. "Something seems…off…but I'm not sure what."

"Uh-oh," Frankie said. "Maybe it's a shark after all!"

"Okay. Now that I've seen it closer, I'm even more convinced that it's a dolphin," Draculaura said. "But—it doesn't seem like it's having fun. It seems kind of…stressed."

"How can you tell?" asked Clawdeen.

"It's swimming *so* fast," Draculaura replied. "Like it's trying to escape or something."

"Escape from what?" Frankie said.

"I don't know," Drac said. "But did you notice how it keeps slapping the water with its tail? It seems upset."

"Yeah…" Cleo said slowly. "I see it too."

Draculaura shivered, even though the water still felt warm. *Must be that cool breeze,* she thought. Then, a sudden flapping movement near her face caught her eye. It wasn't a bird, though. It was—

Draculaura lunged and grabbed on to a piece of damp, wrinkled paper. "Ghouls!" she cried. "What's this?"

"Trash, probably," Clawdeen said with a frown. "Some Normies are total litterbugs."

"It—it's a poster or something!" Draculaura exclaimed. She read the sign aloud. "*Warning.*

Tropical cyclone approaching. Avoid the ocean until further notice."

And there was a small, wavy symbol at the bottom of the page.

Where have I seen that symbol before? Draculaura wondered. "Does this look familiar to you ghouls?" she asked, tapping the symbol with her finger.

The ghouls stared at the sign for a long moment. "I know!" Cleo said. "Wasn't there a symbol like that in Lagoona's e-mail?"

"Maybe!" Draculaura said, getting more excited by the minute. "What if *Lagoona* made this sign? And posted it to warn Normies about the tropical cyclone?"

"What is a tropical cyclone, anyway?" Cleo asked. "I've never heard of that before."

"They're rare—but they can be dangerous," Frankie replied, shouting over the brewing storm. The wind, though, was so strong that the other ghouls heard only one word: *dangerous*.

"Do you think that could be why the dolphin was acting strange?" asked Draculaura.

But before the other ghouls could answer, Clawdeen suddenly yelled out, "I see it!" She pointed at the horizon, where a tall and ominous funnel cloud seemed to materialize from the depths of the ocean. It was swirling faster and faster, zooming across the waves. The winds were even stronger now, whipping the ghouls' wet hair across their scu-boo masks and making it hard to see.

"Now, the ocean is *not* my specialty, but I'd say this looks bad," Cleo said urgently. "Very, very bad."

"I agree," Draculaura replied. "Let's get out of here."

"Where are we going?" Frankie asked.

"Back to Monster High," Draculaura said firmly. "It's the only way. We'll wait out the storm and hopefully when we come back, the cyclone will be gone. Maybe we can find that dolphin again— or someone else who can tell us about Lagoona."

Draculaura reached into the secret pocket of her wetsuit and pulled out the Skullette. She held it out for her ghoulfriends to grab hold of—but the wind yanked it from her fingers. It fell into the sea with a splash!

"No!" Draculaura cried.

Without even bothering to adjust her scu-boo mask, she dove after the Skullette. It was hard to see now; the strong tide was picking up broken bits of shells and tiny grains of sand, swirling them together so that the water appeared thick and murky. Luckily, though, the Skullette glinted and caught Draculaura's eye. Draculaura grabbed it and clutched it in her fist. Then she surfaced and took a deep breath, filling her lungs with air. "Ghouls! I got it!" she cried.

But in the short time she'd been underwater, the tide had carried her friends even farther away.

The cyclone was still approaching—and it was moving fast.

Draculaura knew two things for certain:

She had to get to her ghoulfriends.

And they all had to get out of there!

CHAPTER 9

Swim closer!"

Frankie's voice echoed faintly over the crashing of the waves. Draculaura used every last ounce of her energy and every bit of her strength to swim through the churning waters. The cyclone picked up strength and speed as it tore across the surface of the ocean.

But that same current that was making it so hard for Draculaura to swim was pulling her friends even farther out to sea. "Fight the current!" she screamed. The fierce wind seemed to pull the words from her mouth and throw them away. There was no indication that the other ghouls had heard her—or could even see her as the white-capped waves rose higher and higher.

Draculaura's arms and legs ached from the effort of swimming in such rough seas, but she wasn't about to give up. She reached down deep for one last burst of energy—and that inspired a new idea.

Swim under the waves, she thought suddenly. *Don't fight against them. Go under them.*

Why hadn't it occurred to her before?

Well, it would be scary, for starters. The water was rough beneath the surface too—and murky enough that it would be hard for Draculaura to see where she was swimming. She would also run the risk of losing sight of her ghoulfriends altogether—a thought so scary Draculaura had to push it from her mind. After all, she could just as easily lose them if the cyclone got to them before she did.

I'm on my way, Draculaura thought with determination.

She had to try, after all. It was the only thing she could do.

Draculaura checked her oxygen tank, took a deep breath, and plunged under the water. Her muscles burned, but that didn't stop her from pulling herself through the cloudy, churning ocean. Draculaura kicked and kicked and kicked until finally, she *had* to surface. She had to know where she was, where the tropical cyclone was, where her ghoulfriends were—

"Draculaura!"

The sound of Cleo's voice filled her ears before Draculaura had a chance to wipe the water off her mask. It was enough, in that moment, to hear her ghoulfriend's voice. If nothing else, it told

Draculaura that she was close enough to hear Cleo over the whipping wind. Draculaura opened her mouth to call back—but a huge wave surprised her, crashing over her head and filling her mouth with salt water.

Dragged beneath the waves, Draculaura struggled to pull herself back to the surface. She finally rose above the water, still sputtering and trying to catch her breath. She glanced around and saw that Cleo was just a few feet away.

"Cleo! I'm coming!" Draculaura said. It was so hard to swim those last few feet, but somehow Draculaura managed to do it. She hated to admit it, but she was exhausted—just as the swirling ocean demanded more and more from her.

Cleo seemed to understand. "Hold on to my arm," she said. "My life vest can keep us both afloat."

"Where are Frankie and Clawdeen?" Draculaura finally managed to ask.

Cleo pointed; Draculaura looked in that

direction and saw her ghoulfriends bobbing together on the rough water. "They tried to dive beneath one of those big waves—but the undercurrent dragged them that way," Cleo explained. "I've been trying to swim toward them, but they're just getting farther and farther away."

"That's because the current is pulling them toward the tropical cyclone," Draculaura said grimly. "We've got to get out of here before it gets worse."

"And it looks like it's about to get a *lot* worse," Cleo said anxiously. The tropical cyclone was bearing down on them fast; Draculaura was worried too. If they didn't reach Frankie and Clawdeen soon—

Stop, Draculaura told herself. *Don't even think it.*

"Let's go," Draculaura urged Cleo. "Kick, kick, kick as hard as you can!"

With both ghouls kicking in rhythm, they were finally able to propel themselves through the rough waters. Twenty feet—fifteen feet—ten feet to go—

"Frankie! Clawdeen!" Cleo screamed, trying to be heard over the roaring water and howling winds.

Seven feet—

"We're almost there!" Draculaura cried.

"The Skullette!" Frankie yelled back.

Five feet—

"I've got it!" Drac replied.

Three feet—

They were close enough now that Draculaura and Cleo could reach out far and grab hold of Clawdeen and Frankie. But first, Draculaura had to get the Skullette. She wanted to be ready to transport out of there the instant all four ghouls could touch it.

Another enormous wave swelled, crested, and crashed over the ghoulfriends. Draculaura pressed her clenched fist, with the Skullette tucked inside it, against her heart. She would do anything to protect the Skullette. Luckily, Cleo kept a tight hold on Drac's other arm to keep her from being carried away with the wave. But now the gap had opened up again. Draculaura and Cleo had to swim another fifteen feet to reach their ghoulfriends.

How much longer can this go on? Draculaura thought. She tried to muster her strength. She remembered all the obstacles she had already faced, all the struggles on the way to starting Monster High, and knew that she would never, ever give up.

No matter what.

Kick. Kick. Kick, Draculaura thought, again and again and again, until finally she and Cleo were close enough to grab on to Clawdeen's and Frankie's arms. The four ghouls held one another as tightly as they could, and Draculaura knew that they wouldn't ever let go. Not for anything.

Overhead, the sky crackled. Blinding bolts of lightning leaped from cloud to cloud; it was only a matter of time, Draculaura knew, before one of them hit the water.

But we'll be long gone before that happens, she pledged.

With the Skullette still clenched in her fist, Draculaura held out her hand. She gingerly opened her fingers so the other ghouls could grab hold of the Skullette too.

The massive funnel cloud was so close, but all Draculaura had to do was say the words.

"Monster High—Exsto—"

Whoosh!

But it wasn't the Monster Mapalogue that plucked the ghouls from the raging waters.

It was the tropical cyclone!

The funnel cloud sucked them up, whirling the

ghouls in an endless spin as it traveled across the ocean. Draculaura slammed her eyes shut and tried to hold on as tightly as she could. But she was no match for the ferocious storm.

None of them were.

CHAPTER 10

It took several minutes for Draculaura's head to stop spinning. She was pretty sure she wasn't moving—the ground under her felt strong and solid—but every time she opened her eyes, the bright-blue sky swirled by in a speeding blur. At last, though, the world seemed to slow down as Draculaura's dizziness faded. She pushed herself up to a sitting position, blinked, and looked around.

Draculaura wasn't quite sure where she was,

but she knew one thing: She was nowhere near the ocean. There was no sign of water anywhere, for that matter. Just a vast expanse of dry, dusty dirt for as far as she could see.

There's plenty of time to worry about that later, Draculaura told herself. *Right now, I've got to find my ghoulfriends.*

Draculaura stood up and used her hand to shield her eyes from the relentless sun. "Frankie!" she called. "Clawdeen! Cleo!"

There was no response.

"Frankie! Clawdeen! Cleo!"

Draculaura waited, straining her ears to hear anything.

Still nothing.

"Frankie! Clawdeen! Cleooooooooooooooo!"

"Draculaura!"

"Over here!"

"Ghouls!" Draculaura cried in excitement. "Where are you?"

Suddenly, she saw Frankie's head pop up from behind a scrubby bush. "This way, Drac! We've been looking for you."

Draculaura hurried over and pulled her ghoul-friends into an enormous hug. "I was so worried I wouldn't find you," she said. "Is everybody okay?"

"Better than okay," Frankie announced. She held up both hands and wiggled all her fingers. "If I hadn't been wearing my super-strong wet-suit, I would've lost a body part for sure!"

All the ghouls laughed—until Draculaura gasped, startling everyone. Then she spun around and raced away.

"Drac! Draculaura! What's wrong?" Clawdeen called as the other ghouls chased after her.

"It's lost!" Draculaura cried. "The Skullette! It's gone!"

She fell to her knees and started digging in the dry red dirt. Dusty clouds rose around her, making Draculaura cough—but she just dug deeper.

Frankie, Clawdeen, and Cleo all exchanged a worried glance.

"It was in my hand—I was holding it so tight!" Draculaura continued in a panic. "It *has* to be here—help me look! It can't be far!"

Frankie knelt down beside Draculaura and placed her hand on Drac's shoulder. "Hey," she said in a quiet voice. "Maybe we should—"

"I have to find it," Draculaura interrupted her. "How else are we going to get home?"

Draculaura's frantic question hung in the air—and made her start digging even harder.

"Listen, ghoul," Clawdeen began. "This is not your fault, okay? Nobody could've held on to the Skullette during that storm."

Draculaura shook her head. "It's our only way home," she said. "We *have* to find it!"

"Clawdeen is right," Cleo said firmly. "The

important thing is that we're together. So what if the Skullette is missing? We'll figure out something else! That's what monsters do!"

Draculaura stopped digging. She covered her face with her dusty hands. "I'm so sorry, ghouls," she groaned. "This is awful. And it's all my fault!"

"No—it was the storm's fault," Frankie reminded her. "We don't even know where we are. There's no sign of the ocean. Obviously the storm was strong enough to blow us into—into—"

"The middle of nowhere?" Clawdeen said with a big sigh.

"Something like that," Frankie said, nodding.

"This is the worst," Draculaura said. "Now we're even farther from Lagoona. And how are we going to get home again? Dad will be worried sick—"

"Your dad!" Cleo suggested suddenly. "Do you think he could fly to us?"

Draculaura blinked. "I don't know," she said. "That would be a really long trip. Plus, my dad thinks we're in the middle of the ocean—not, um, wherever we are."

"If we could find Lagoona," Frankie said slowly, "we could use her Monster Web to send a message to Mr. D. I'm sure he'd be able to find a way to bring us back to Monster High."

"That's a clawesome idea!" cheered Clawdeen. "Don't forget, Mr. D. is the one who gave us the Monster Mapalogue. He'll definitely be able to think of something."

Thinking of the Monster Mapalogue made Draculaura feel even worse. "Ugh," she groaned. "The Monster Mapalogue has been a treasured monster heirloom for millennia—and now it's ruined forever! You can't use it without the Skullette!"

"Don't talk like that," Clawdeen replied. "We might still be able to find the Skullette. But I agree with Frankie and Cleo. We can't spend too much time searching for it right now. We have bigger problems to figure out."

"Like where, exactly, we are," Frankie spoke up. She turned to Cleo. "You've spent your entire life in the desert—does any of this look familiar?"

Cleo shook her head. "Sorry, ghoul," she replied. "My desert is basically golden sand and shadowy dunes. I don't see even one tiny monument to my family out here. It's like another world!"

"I suppose that would've been too much to hope for," Frankie said.

Draculaura stared at the unusual landscape around her. The red dirt...the stunted, scrubby plants...the rocky mesas...

Suddenly, her eyes lit up. "I know!" she exclaimed. "We must be in the Outback!"

"Out back of what?" Cleo asked in confusion.

"No, it's called the Outback," Draculaura

explained. "It's an area Down Unda, near the Great Barrier Reef. I read about it in my book. It can be extremely dangerous here—the heat is relentless! We really need to get back to the ocean and the Great Barrier Reef."

"That's not all we need," Cleo said. "I learned a thing or two from a lifetime in the desert. And I don't know if we'll be able to make it to the Great Barrier Reef without finding an oasis—or at least some water and shade—on the way."

"Look at these bushes, though," Clawdeen pointed out. "They're so short and stubby. They barely provide enough shade for my shoe, let alone all four of us."

"Probably because there's not enough water here for them to grow bigger," Draculaura said.

"Just because we can't see water doesn't mean we can't find it," Cleo told the ghouls. She knelt down and studied the dirt carefully for a few minutes.

What is she looking for? Draculaura wondered. But Cleo was studying the ground with such intense concentration that Drac didn't want to disturb her.

"Ah, here we go," Cleo said suddenly as her fingers traced one of the cracks in the red dirt. "Follow me!"

Cleo charged off, with the other ghouls right behind her. Draculaura couldn't tell if Cleo was following a faint trail in the dirt or the network of cracks that spread across the barren landscape. Either way, though, Cleo seemed completely confident.

As they moved through the sunny Outback, Draculaura couldn't help noticing that it was strangely beautiful. The sun was beating down hard, though, and Drac was starting to feel a little light- headed. One look at Clawdeen told Drac that her friend felt the same way. *I hope we find water soon,* Draculaura worried. *I'm not sure how long Clawdeen can last without it.*

Cleo stopped abruptly; Draculaura had to move to the side to avoid running into her.

"See that ridge ahead?" asked Cleo. "There should be a freshwater lake on the other side of it."

"How do you know?" asked Clawdeen as she pushed her thick hair back from her face.

"Those cracks in the dirt aren't just cracks," Cleo explained. "They're tributaries—like itty-bitty streams. They dried up because of how small they were, which made it easy for the water in them to evaporate. But following the cracks should lead us to the source, which will have plenty of fresh water for us to drink."

"Ghoul, you're a genius!" Frankie said approvingly.

"Anything to help my best ghoulfriends! Even getting a little too up close and personal with dirt," answered Cleo cheerfully.

Then Frankie turned to Clawdeen. "You can make it—we're almost there."

Clawdeen flashed a smile. "Can't wait," she replied. "Because this ghoul is parched."

"Not for long!" Cleo sang out as the ghouls hiked up the ridge. But when they reached the top, her grin faded. "I—I—" she stammered. She didn't need to say anything, though. The ghouls could see for themselves that there wasn't a single drop of water for them to drink.

"It's a dry lake bed," Draculaura said. "An empty crater now that all the water has dried up."

"I'm so sorry, ghouls," Cleo said. "I expected there to be a lake here. I let you down."

Draculaura wrapped her arm around Cleo's shoulders and gave her a quick hug. "No you didn't," Draculaura reassured her. "How could you know?"

"Actually..." Frankie began.

When the ghouls turned to look at her, they saw sparks twinkling near the bolts in her neck.

"We might be in the perfect spot to find fresh

water!" Frankie announced. She dropped her backpack on the ground and started rummaging in it.

Draculaura couldn't help smiling. Those sparks flying from Frankie's bolts were a good sign. No—they were a *great* sign!

"I present to you my custom-built, super-charged water-finding invention!" Frankie said excitedly as she pulled a thin silver rod out of her backpack.

Clawdeen and Draculaura recognized it right away. They started to cheer, but Cleo just looked confused. "What *is* that, some sort of scepter?" she asked.

"It's just a little something Frankie invented while we were trying to rescue you," Draculaura replied.

"But what does it do?" said Cleo.

Draculaura smiled mysteriously. "Prepare to be ugh-mazed!"

"Hold this, please," Frankie said as she passed the stick to Draculaura. Then she rubbed her hands together until shimmery sparks jumped from her fingertips. As soon as Draculaura gave the stick back to Frankie, it started to quiver and jerk her forward.

"Voltageous!" Frankie cheered. "Ghouls, we are *definitely* in the right place!"

"But—" Cleo began.

Before she could utter another word, Frankie plunged the stick into the ground.

Whooosh!

An enormous fountain of clean, clear water sprang up from the dry dirt!

CHAPTER 11

"A*hhhhhh!*" the ghouls screamed as they jumped out of the way. The cool mist felt refreshing on their faces.

"How did you do that?" Cleo asked in amazement.

"This isn't an ordinary silver stick," Frankie explained. "It has a copper core that conducts electricity and helps it find water. And with a little extra power, it can dig straight down until it reaches a water source underground."

"We would've built statues to you back in ancient Egypt!" Cleo marveled.

"Grab your canteens, ghouls!" Clawdeen said. "Let's fill 'em up!"

The ghouls drank their fill of the water Cleo and Frankie had found. Despite the heat of the day, the water was surprisingly cold and refreshing.

"It must've been really far underground," Cleo said as she paused to refill her canteen.

"That's such a crazy thought," Draculaura said. "It's so dry and dusty up here—but all this fresh water was flowing just beneath the surface."

"Let's climb back up to the ridge. Then we can figure out what to do next," Clawdeen suggested as she splashed some water on her face.

Back on the ridge, the girls watched as the fountain slowed.

"I wish this ridge were high enough that we could see the ocean from here," Draculaura said.

"At least then we'd know if we're heading in the right direction."

"But we shouldn't just charge off," Clawdeen spoke up. "What if we go the wrong way and end up deeper into the Outback? We could get even more lost!"

"And our full canteens will last us only so long," Frankie reminded them.

Draculaura turned to her. "Frankie," she began. "What about your invention? Do you think it could lead us to the ocean?"

"Well—sure. I guess," Frankie replied, deep in thought. "The only problem is that we wouldn't really know if it was leading us to the ocean until we got there. It could lead us to a totally different water source."

"Is that the worst thing that could happen?" Clawdeen asked. "At least we could fill our canteens again! I wonder if..."

"What?" Draculaura asked. There was a look of deep curiosity on Clawdeen's face, like she was trying to figure something out, and Draculaura couldn't wait to hear what her ghoulfriend had to say.

"Do you think it's possible the cyclone left a trail when it crossed over land?" Clawdeen asked. "If we could find any sign of it, we could follow the trail. It would lead us right back to the ocean."

"That's possible," Frankie said. "Most of the time, tropical cyclones will fizzle out when they reach land—but sometimes the clouds and high winds can travel over land for hundreds of miles."

"I know!" Draculaura exclaimed. "If we find a trail to follow—even a couple signs or clues—we can use Frankie's invention to confirm that we're heading in the direction of the water!"

"Voltageous!" Frankie cheered as she gave Draculaura a high five.

"Let's split up," Clawdeen suggested. "I mean, we should always stay in eyesight, but we can cover more ground if we move in different directions. And every few minutes, we can yell our names so we know we're all nearby."

"I have a question," Cleo spoke up. "What kind of clues, exactly, are you talking about?"

"Well, clumps of seaweed, for starters," Frankie replied. "Broken branches or uprooted plants might be a sign that the tropical cyclone passed over them. Sometimes a cyclone can even make it rain fish over land."

"*What?*" Cleo burst out loudly. The other ghouls looked at her, and she grinned. "Sorry, ghouls… it didn't rain fish where I grew up. It was the desert…it didn't rain, period!"

The four ghouls all burst out laughing and then sighed, enjoying the relief. "Honestly, I wouldn't mind a fish rainstorm if it could show us how to get back to the Great Barrier Reef," Clawdeen replied. "Good luck, ghouls. Remember, there's no clue too small!"

The ghouls split up, each exploring a different side of the basin that was still filling with water. At first, Draculaura saw nothing but dust, dirt, and scrubby little plants. The earth was so dry that she and her ghoulfriends didn't even leave footprints. Apart from the sound of water flowing through the fountain, the Outback was eerily quiet. Every few minutes, the ghouls would call to one another, their voices echoing off the dusty landscape.

Suddenly, a shriek of excitement pierced the silence.

"Ghouls! I found something!" Cleo cried.

Draculaura ran to the other side of the basin, where she found Cleo holding up several long strands of delicate sea grass. And they were still damp!

"These must be from the Great Barrier Reef!"

Draculaura exclaimed. "And the only possible explanation—"

"Is that the cyclone carried them here!" Frankie finished for her. Frankie grabbed her invention and said, "Come on—let's go!"

"But which direction?" asked Clawdeen.

"I'm not exactly sure," Frankie admitted. "We might have some false starts. But at least we know that the cyclone passed over this side of the basin. If my invention starts giving us a strong signal of water, we'll know we're going the right way."

"And if it doesn't?" asked Cleo.

"Then I guess we'll have to backtrack and try a different direction," Frankie replied. She started rubbing her hands together again so that she could give the silver stick an even more powerful charge.

A small, worried frown crossed Draculaura's face. It wasn't the worst plan—but there was still a lot that could go wrong.

But what other option did they have?

Judging from the uneasy silence, the other ghouls seemed to share her concerns. They walked on for several feet before Draculaura finally spoke. "Any signs from your invention, Frankie?"

Frankie nodded. "It's definitely picking up on underground water," she replied. "I really think we're on the right track."

"That's fangtastic!" Draculaura said. "I'm kind of worried about how far we are from the ocean. It could take us *days* to walk that far."

"Days?" Clawdeen repeated. "I didn't think of that."

"What are we going to eat?" Cleo wondered.

Draculaura stared at the barren landscape all around them and shook her head. "I honestly don't know," she replied. "We'll have to—Hey, what's that?"

The ghouls followed Draculaura's gaze to the other side of the basin, where a dusty cloud had appeared. As they watched, the cloud grew larger—and closer.

"That looks like a sandstorm!" Cleo said. "We have them all the time in the desert. Strong winds pick up the sand and blow it so hard that you can't see anything at all. Really makes a mess of your eyeliner when you get all that sand in your eyes..."

"Maybe it's a dust storm," Frankie suggested.

"Oh no—not another storm!" Clawdeen groaned. "My hair may never recover!"

"I'm not sure it's a storm," Draculaura said. "I don't feel any wind. Not even a little breeze."

"Neither do I," Frankie said.

"Then what could it be?" asked Cleo.

Draculaura squinted, trying to get a better look. Suddenly, she became aware of something else: The ground—it was trembling. Ripples formed in the little lake, shimmering with every pulsing motion that shook the ground. If she didn't know better, she'd think a herd of—

"Brumbies!" Draculaura yelled.

The other ghouls turned to her. "Brum-*what?*" asked Clawdeen, looking puzzled.

Draculaura was beaming. "Brumbies are wild horses that graze in the Outback!" she explained. "They must've seen the fountain spring up."

"So you think they came to drink the water?" Cleo said.

"Yes," Draculaura replied. "And hopefully they'll be our rides!"

The ghouls watched in silence, hardly daring to move, as dozens of beautiful horses approached the pool. As the dust settled, the majestic creatures bent their long necks and drank deeply from the cool, clear water. There were black brumbies and brown brumbies, brumbies the color of honey, and dappled brumbies with mottled spots.

"Some brumbies are tamer than others," Drac whispered to the other ghouls. "Over the years, domesticated horses would sometimes escape from ranches or farms. They formed wild herds in the Outback and have lived freely ever since. But according to *The Wundas of Down Unda*, some of them still remember their training."

"So now we knew what we have to do," Frankie whispered back. "Figure out which brumbies are still tame—and hitch a ride back to the Great Barrier Reef."

"Without spooking the wild ones and making the whole herd gallop away like a bunch of werepups," added Clawdeen.

"They seem pretty calm right now," said Draculaura. "Let's try to approach them. Remember, slow and steady. No sudden movements."

"Lesson number one of Monster Rescue: no sudden movements, ever," joked Clawdeen.

The ghouls tried to stifle their laughter for a

moment before Cleo interrupted. "Okay, ghouls! Focus!"

Staying low to the ground, the ghouls crept toward the brumbies. Draculaura couldn't take her eyes off the herd. If there weren't so much at stake, she would've been perfectly happy just to watch them. But the ghouls had to get back to the ocean—the sooner, the better.

A brumby near the edge of the herd looked up from the water and caught Draculaura's eye. It tilted its head to the side as Draculaura and the brumby gazed at each other. When Drac inched forward, the brumby didn't move away. It didn't even flinch.

That's encouraging, Draculaura thought. She continued to move closer until she was a few inches away. Then she gradually extended her arm, palm up, toward the brumby.

Draculaura held her breath as she waited to

see how the brumby would respond. Would it rear back? Would it gallop away?

The brumby blinked its big brown eyes. Then it leaned down and sniffed Draculaura's hand!

Draculaura rubbed the brumby's nose and scratched the white star-shaped mark between its eyes. Then she gestured for Cleo, Clawdeen, and Frankie to find their own brumbies. Drac was grateful that her ghoulfriends were being so cautious. If the herd panicked and bolted when they were so close to success, it would be a catastrophe!

Soon Cleo and Clawdeen found a pair of tame brumbies. Just Frankie was left. But she was at a disadvantage; her supercharged invention was still crackling, and it made all the brumbies anxious. Draculaura understood why Frankie didn't want to stash the invention in her backpack. Keeping it close was the best way for the ghouls to know if they were on the right route to the ocean. But if the stick prevented Frankie from riding a brumby to the coast, they'd have no choice but to put her invention away—and hope they were heading in the right direction.

Draculaura watched as Frankie approached a gray brumby with a gleaming black mane. The brumby took one look at the silver stick, snorted, and bolted away. When Frankie looked over at Draculaura and shrugged helplessly, Drac knew exactly what she had to do. She gestured at the invention, then pointed at Frankie's bag. Frankie nodded to show that she understood. She hid the silver stick, then approached another brumby. And this one let her get close!

Draculaura smiled, then started stroking her brumby's mane. "Do you think you could give me a ride?" Draculaura asked. She had no idea if the brumby could understand her, but it seemed polite to ask. When the brumby still didn't bolt, Draculaura hoisted herself up onto its back.

After the other ghouls had mounted their brumbies, Draculaura nodded at them. It was time to go!

"Can you take us to the ocean?" Draculaura asked. The brumby whickered softly in response. Draculaura pressed her knees against the brumby's sides and held on tight.

The brumby must've remembered what to do when someone wanted to ride. It reared back on its hind legs, then started galloping across the Outback! Draculaura shrieked with glee as her hair streamed behind her. Drac could feel her heart beating in time to the brumby's thundering hooves. Out of the corner of her eye, she saw Cleo first—then Clawdeen—and then Frankie— all holding on just as tightly and, Drac could tell, smiling just as broadly as she was. Riding a wild brumby through the dramatic landscape of the Outback was an adventure the ghouls would remember forever!

For nearly two hours, the ghouls rode the brumbies as the blazing sun crossed the sky. Gradually, the landscape changed. The plants grew taller and greener. There were signs of other creatures—cockatiels and rabbits, snakes and lizards, dingoes and kangaroos. And eventually the dusty red dirt gave way to something else: soft, golden sand. Draculaura could hear the ocean before she could see it. The roar of the waves made her even more excited: They were back on track at last!

When the brumbies finally reached the coast, Draculaura was surprised to see that the ferocious storm had completely vanished. Once more, the sky was clear, without a single cloud. The waves were rougher than she remembered from her first visit with Clawdeen, but not nearly as dangerous as they'd been during the tropical cyclone.

Draculaura slid off her brumby and threw her arms around its neck. "Thanks for the ride," she whispered near its ear as she gave it one last hug. The brumby tossed its mane, pawed at the sand, and then began to gallop back in the opposite direction. The other brumbies followed; the ghouls watched until the horses were enveloped in a cloud of dust and then gone from sight.

"Back to the beach!" Cleo cheered as she knelt down and scooped up a handful of sand. "I never thought I'd be this happy to see the ocean again!"

"Me too!" Draculaura replied. "That was a big detour, but at least we're back on track now."

"Yeah," added Clawdeen. "Operation Go Get Lagoona is back in action!"

Draculaura glanced around. Except for the four ghouls, the beach was deserted. "I guess all the Normies are still waiting out the storm," she said.

"They could come back at any moment," Cleo said, a note of worry in her voice.

"You're right. Let's get back to the ocean," Clawdeen said. "Maybe we can find that dolphin again. She might be able to lead us to Lagoona now that the storm is over."

Frankie began inspecting her wetsuit. "Gotta make sure there aren't any rips or tears," she said. "After the day we've had, you can't be too careful."

"I don't want to rush you or anything," Cleo spoke up, "but the weather is getting better and better. I bet the Normies will show up any minute."

"I'll go as fast as I can," Frankie promised.

"Uh, ghouls?" Clawdeen began. "Don't freak or anything, but I think they're already here. Check it out."

When the other ghouls looked out toward the horizon, Draculaura's heart sank. There was someone in the ocean after all. *Where did she come from?* Draculaura wondered. The Normie hadn't been there just moments ago.

Wait a minute, Draculaura thought as she narrowed her eyes. A wave swelled. The figure, crouched on a surfboard, stood up with perfect balance. Her blond hair was streaked with blue highlights that were just a shade darker than her skin—and that was when Draculaura knew.

"Lagoona!" she screamed.

CHAPTER 12

Draculaura, Cleo, Clawdeen, and Frankie raced down to the edge of the ocean, never taking their eyes off the ghoul on the surfboard. The ghoul made it look effortless, even when the wave crested in a rush of swirling foam. About twenty feet from shore, she spotted Drac and her ghoulfriends. She looked alarmed for about half a second—then total excitement flooded her face. She did an aerial 360 on the board, then rode in to shore.

"Draculaura! Ghoulfriend!" she cried. "Is that really you?"

"Lagoona!" Draculaura exclaimed. "At last! This is Clawdeen, and this is Frankie, and—"

"I'm Cleo," Cleo interrupted with a bright smile. "I can't believe we finally found you!"

"And I can't believe you're finally here!" Lagoona said.

"Sorry it took so long," Draculaura said. "We've had a few...obstacles." *And they're not over yet,* Drac thought to herself, but she didn't want to say those words aloud. Lagoona was so happy to see them; Draculaura didn't want to ruin things by telling her about the lost Skullette and the challenge it would be to return to Monster High.

"That's dreadful," Lagoona said. "I'm sorry I missed you when you first arrived. I was surfing—we always try to enjoy the ocean when the Normies aren't around. Oh! That reminds me. Does this belong to you?"

Lagoona unzipped a pocket on her wetsuit and pulled out something that dangled from a thin golden chain. Draculaura blinked in disbelief. "The Skullette! How did you find it?" she exclaimed.

"The chain caught on an edge of the reef near my home," Lagoona explained. "When I saw it, I just *knew* it had to belong to you! What is it, anyway?"

"It's our ticket back to Monster High!" said Draculaura, laughing. "It's part of the Monster Mapalogue, which helps us travel all over the world. I lost it when the cyclone picked us up and, well...it's a long story. I can't boo-lieve this—I never thought I'd see it again!"

"I was starting to think I'd never see *you*!" Lagoona said as she gave Draculaura a big hug. "There aren't any other monsters my age around here. I love my family, but a ghoul needs mates too."

"I know exactly what you mean," Draculaura replied.

"Honestly, I was starting to give up hope," Lagoona continued.

Draculaura's face wrinkled into a frown. "Didn't you get my messages?" she asked.

"Messages?" Lagoona repeated, her eyes wide. She shook her head. "I haven't gotten anything from you since your announcement about the opening of Monster High."

Drac and Frankie exchanged a knowing look. "We really did try to reach you," Drac said. "I don't know why our messages didn't make it through."

"Crikey, that's not your fault," Lagoona assured her. "The Monster Web's been spotty with that storm brewing. It's not very reliable under the best of circumstances, anyway."

"Want me to take a look?" Frankie offered. "I might be able to fix it."

"That would be fintastic!" Lagoona replied. "Of

course, I'll want to stay in touch with my fam when I'm at Monster High."

"And while Frankie fixes your connection to the Monster Web, we can help you pack," Draculaura said. "After all, that's what ghoulfriends are for."

Lagoona started to laugh. "Oh, ghoul, I'm already packed," she said. "I've been ready to go since the moment I heard about Monster High!"

As the other ghouls joined in the laughter, Draculaura smiled. *This,* she thought happily. *This moment is what Monster High is all about.*

"But there is one thing we should do before we leave," Lagoona suggested.

"What?" asked Cleo.

"Catch some waves!" Lagoona announced. "What do you say? Fancy a surfing lesson?"

"From *you*?" Draculaura exclaimed. "Fangtastic!"

"Do you have enough boards for all of us?" asked Clawdeen.

Lagoona laughed. "Does the Blue family have

enough boards!" she said. "Well, there's one for my dad, and one for my mum, and each of my sisters has one, and then my brothers—"

Draculaura and the other ghouls started laughing too.

"Come on," Lagoona said. "Last one in is a silly sea critter!"

We did it, Draculaura thought happily as she splashed into the water with Cleo, Clawdeen, Frankie, and Lagoona. *We found another student— and even more important, we made a new ghoulfriend.*

And that was exactly what Monster High was about!

Did you ♥ reading about
Lagoona's rescue?

Then you'll love reading
MONSTER RESCUE
TRACK DOWN TWYLA!
COMING SOON!